May-lee Chai

TRAINING DAYS

May-lee Chai is the author of eight books, including the memoir *Hapa Girl*, a Kiriyama Prize Notable Book; the novel *Dragon Chica*; and the novel *Tiger Girl*, which won an Asian/ Pacific American Award for Literature. She teaches creative writing and literary translation at San Francisco State University.

First published by GemmaMedia in 2018.

GemmaMedia
230 Commercial Street
Boston MA 02109 USA

www.gemmamedia.com

Printed in the United States of America

978-1-936846-62-7

Library of Congress Cataloging-in-Publication Data

Names: Chai, May-Lee, author.
Title: Training days / May-Lee Chai.
Description: Boston MA : GemmaMedia, 2017. | Series: Gemma
open doors
Identifiers: LCCN 2017040459 | ISBN 9781936846627
Classification: LCC PS3553.H2423 T73 2017 | DDC 813/.54–
dc23 LC record available at https://lccn.loc.gov/2017040459

Cover by Laura Shaw Design

Gemma's Open Doors provide fresh stories, new ideas, and essential resources for young people and adults as they embrace the power of reading and the written word.

Brian Bouldrey
Series Editor

GEMMA

Open Door

For Judy Blume

"If Sally could sing like her father, or even whistle, she wouldn't be in the listener group in music class. It wasn't much fun to mouth the words while everyone else got to sing them. Sometimes Sally would forget to just listen and she would sing too. Then Miss Vickers would ask, 'Sally Freedman . . . are you singing out loud?' and Sally would go back to mouthing the words."

—*Starring Sally J. Freedman as Herself*

Characters

Aunt Mei, pronounced "MAY"

Cindy Van Lenten—Jun-li's classmate

George—Jun-li's Siberian husky

Jeremy—Jun-li's brother, three years
   younger

Jun-li, pronounced "JUN-LEE"—
   eleven-year-old girl

Linda—Jun-li's mother

Madison—Jun-li's cousin, daughter of
   Aunt Mei

Maria Glinbizzi, pronounced "glin-
   BIT-zee"—Jun-li's friend with
   dark, curly hair

Mr. Tralucci, pronounced "trah-LOO-
   chee"—father of one of Jeremy's
   classmates

Nai-nai, pronounced "NYE-NYE"
(rhymes with bye-bye)—Jun-li's
grandmother

Sean, pronounced "SHAHN"—
Maria's brother, one year younger

Uncle Roger—Aunt Mei's husband,
father of Madison and the twins

Walter—Jun-li's dad, brother of Uncle
Roger

Ye-ye, pronounced "YEH-YEH"—
Jun-li's grandfather

CHAPTER 1

"Did you get yours yet?" Maria asked. She pulled the package out of her dresser. It was her new training bra. It was white and stretchy and had two pink rosebuds sewn between the cups.

I felt my cheeks grow hot. I looked down so my hair fell in front of my face, like looking at the bra was so interesting, I just couldn't look up again. "My mother says we're going to wait till the end of the summer."

"That's in case you grow," Maria said. "That's what my mother was worried about, too. But my dad said she'd better hurry up. Can you believe it? At the dinner table. In front of Sean."

"Oh my god. I can't believe your

dad said that." I was suddenly thankful my father was too busy to ever notice anything I was doing.

"I know," she said. Maria twisted one of her long, dark, curly locks around her index finger. "That's why I'm hiding it. I think Sean and his stupid friends were looking through my stuff."

"What a jerk," I said.

"He's a pervert," Maria agreed.

Maria's brother was only a year behind us in school. Sometimes I'd see Sean in the hallway, waiting with his friends to go to the bathroom or lining up in front of the drinking fountain. At Maria's house, he was like a little kid, sitting in front of the TV, shooting a toy gun at the Klingons, *pew pew pew*!

But at school, the boys he hung out with whistled in the halls and called girls names.

I was glad my brother, Jeremy, was three years younger. It made him more manageable.

At least when we started junior high in September, Sean would still be in elementary school, and we wouldn't have to worry about him for a year.

"Look, Jun-li, do you wanna guess where it was made?" Maria pulled the bra's tag up so that I could see. In very clear red letters it said, MADE IN R.O.C.

Suddenly, my face burned anew. Republic of China. I knew exactly where that was on the map. It was a small island in the sea next to the bigger mainland. Dad had lived there as a

3

boy, but I couldn't picture him there. Instead, I thought of my grandparents who'd lived in Taipei before coming to America five years ago. Ye-ye always dressed up in his suit when we went out to eat dinner as a family, and Nai-nai wore her Chinese-style dresses in New York. Still, the image came to me of dozens of old women who looked just like my grandmother hunched over sewing machines, sewing little bras for American girls. I felt ashamed, although I did not know why. I braced myself for whatever Maria would say. Would she think my family had made her bra?

"*Rock*," she pronounced. "Isn't that funny? What kind of country is that?"

Poor Maria, I thought, relieved.

But then I realized that maybe this was secretly why we were friends. I could feel safe with her. I was always one step ahead.

"Yeah," I said. "It's like *Rocky* the movie." I laughed. "Yo, Adrian!" I called in my best Rocky voice.

"Yeah, yeah, it's just like that," she said, and she snatched the bra and put it over her shirt, her fists in the cups. "Yo, Adrian!" she called to herself, and then pranced around. Maybe she was supposed to be Adrian, or just some woman with a bra, something ridiculous like that. We both laughed and laughed until Maria farted and then she turned red and ran outside her room, then back inside, and farted again. We both rolled on her carpet, hysterical.

CHAPTER 2

I was still on Nancy Drew 43: *The Mystery of the 99 Steps*, and the muggy days in northern New Jersey stretched taffy-slow from one Good Humor truck to the next.

That summer, my father was under contract to write a new textbook, and he was stressed-out, tense and angry all the time. There were pages of the book spread on the dining room table, on the folding table Dad had set up in the living room, and on the ping-pong table in the basement. Jeremy and I weren't allowed to go into the rooms where Dad was working, so there was no ping-pong for us all summer.

At least this work meant Mom and Dad were arguing less than usual. In fact, they weren't really talking much at all. Dad was busy typing and Mom was busy teaching summer school.

I hadn't thought about getting my bra until Maria brought it up. Then I felt left behind. A new anxiety crept up on me.

But when I asked Mom if we could get mine, Mom said she was too busy to go shopping for school clothes. She was teaching night classes and was gone most evenings. On the weekends, she had papers to grade or meetings to attend.

"But Maria Glinbizzi's mother already bought hers," I said.

Mom clicked her tongue against her teeth. "I didn't need a bra until I was thirteen."

I wanted to add that she hadn't grown up in America, but in Canada, far away. Who knew what was normal there? But I held my tongue.

The thing I wanted most was to be just like my friends in school. I knew this meant that I should do the things they did. My parents did not always understand. Neither of my parents had been born in America, and sometimes I wondered if that was why they argued so much. My friends' parents seemed to argue less, but it was hard to say. Sometimes parents hid things in front of other peoples' kids. My parents did that.

The handouts for junior high were clear. The list of things we had to buy before we started in the fall was printed in bold: book covers, No. 2 pencils, three-ring binders with "No Imagery on the Cover," gym shorts and T-shirts in school colors, the right kind of sneakers (no black soles that would scuff the gym floors), and "gender-appropriate underwear." And then in parentheses, it was spelled out so everyone knew what that meant: bras for girls and jockstraps for boys. I pointed this line out to Mom. She glanced at the sheet and said, "Oh, bother."

Mom later handed me the Sears catalog with the corner turned down on the page for training bras. There were three kinds, all of them as white as a starched nurse's uniform. One had a tiny pink-and-blue tennis racket between the cups, one had a white daisy, and one was plain.

Mom was going to order one from the catalog, but then she said, "You're probably going to need to try it on first." And she sighed, as though I were becoming one more burden she had to deal with in the day. You'd have thought I was like my cousin Madison the time she got ringworm. Mom's voice sounded like I had caught some illness that could spread. I didn't tell that to Maria, though.

I hadn't thought much about bras up till this point. My chest was flat and straight, and my belly was round and smooth and still pressed against my shirts. I wondered if my lack of breasts might be due to the fact that I was Chinese (no one said *Taiwanese* in those days). But I had no other Chinese classmates, no one to compare myself to except my mother, who always seemed perfect in her womanhood, the opposite of me. I had no way to tell if I was normal.

But when I talked to Cindy Van Lenten, I noticed she was even flatter than I was—and six months older. I felt some relief. I asked her straight up if she was going to try to do without, but Cindy shook her head gravely. It was too risky, she said. If you didn't wear a training bra in gym class, for example, and your boobs started to come in, they could grow crooked, and they'd be

11

two different sizes. They would never be normal when you grew up, she said, unless your training bra was there to press them into place. That's what the orientation packet meant. They hadn't fully explained because they didn't want to scare us.

I nodded, because that seemed right. Adults were just like that. They only ever said half of what they meant.

CHAPTER 3

Mom told Aunt Mei about my needing a training bra. I couldn't believe my ears, the way she just blurted it out. I thought my mother would have had a clue. After all, Mom had been my age once. But adults were always disappointing me.

It was late in the summer. Mom's night classes were finally over, so we'd gone to pick up Madison to play at our house, but Madison was still at her swimming lesson. Aunt Mei let us in to wait. She said the twins were finally sleeping. We all sat down in the living room, Mom on the piano bench and me on the armchair and Aunt Mei on the rocker. There were laundry baskets on the sofa and a diaper genie in the corner. For the first time, the house didn't smell like Madison's rabbit. It smelled worse.

"I was just soaking myself," Aunt Mei said. She unbuttoned her blouse and I saw her nursing bra. It was bright white and thick, with snaps and triangular flaps that opened. She put wet, cold Lipton tea bags through the openings, sighing.

"Old wives' trick, my mom used to say." She laughed, a short bark, like a seal.

Then she closed her eyes and leaned her head against the back of the rocking chair.

"I bottle-fed Jun-li," Mom volunteered. "I wanted to breastfeed her, but I was under a lot of stress. I lost all my milk." (I kept waiting for her to add, "And she turned out all right," as she had at home, when she'd told my brother and me this story.) "But when Jeremy came along, I was able to breastfeed a full six months. And he had quite the appetite."

"My mother breastfed me until I was almost four years old," Aunt Mei said with her eyes closed. She rocked back and forth, back and forth.

"Oh, is that so?"

"Mom was old-school. Everything had to be the way her mother had done things. And my grandmother, Po-po, was a tyrant. I remember when I was growing up, Mom and me had to scrub the floors on our hands and knees. Po-po said it was the only way to really get the dirt. She lived to be ninety-seven, if you can believe it. Outlived Mom by five years."

"Did I meet your grandmother at the wedding?"

"That was her in the wheelchair with the oxygen tank." Aunt Mei let out another seal-bark laugh. "I don't think she knew who I was anymore. Kept calling me by my mom's name. Really, she took care of me more than my mother did. She lived with us the whole time I was growing up so Mom could work."

"When did your father die?"

"Dad died of a heart attack before I was born. I always blamed all my problems on his dying. If I'd grown up with a father figure. A father, I mean.

If I'd gotten used to having a man in the house, maybe I'd understand them better."

"No," Mom said. "Nothing prepares you. Nothing helps. I had a father and two brothers."

"And no mother. You had to raise yourself."

"I had no training for life. It's true," Mom said.

Slumped into the rocking chair, Aunt Mei looked as though she were asleep. But her right hand was moving, patting at the tea bags, adjusting them, prodding them. The rest of her body just lay there, dead.

I looked away quickly and held my book in front of my nose, but I couldn't focus on the words on the page. Seeing

17

Aunt Mei prone and lifeless made me nervous, made my heart beat too fast. I wasn't sure who I could share this story with. Not Jeremy—he was a boy. And not Madison, who was too young. But it also didn't seem like something Cindy Van Lenten or Maria Glinbizzi would appreciate. We talked about the usual things, like TV shows and movies and books. Or we gossiped about other kids at school and weird things teachers had said or done when they thought we weren't looking. I couldn't see how to bring in such a separate, adult experience.

Madison's pet bunny hopped past the living room door and slipped behind the sofa. I saw the curtains move and knew it was creeping deeper and deeper into hiding. It would chew on power cords and the underpart of the couch. I knew because Madison had told me about her parents' fights. Aunt Mei had threatened to get rid of it after coming home and finding a giant hole in the middle of a cushion. White stuffing like snowflakes had been spread about the carpet.

"We're going to buy Jun-li a training bra this summer," Mom told Aunt Mei.

All the heat in my body rushed to my face. I looked daggers at my mother, but she was folding the laundry from one of the baskets. She didn't look at me once as she smoothed washcloths against the arm of the sofa.

"Time flies," Aunt Mei said.

I wanted to die right there. It was one thing for Aunt Mei to mess with her own nursing bra. It was another when they were talking about my training bra!

CHAPTER 4

Miraculously, Uncle Roger and Madison came back from the Y. I heard the car pull up into the driveway. Madison ran inside. Her towel was over her shoulder. Her hair was still damp.

"Don't wake the babies," Aunt Mei hissed, and Madison stopped in her tracks.

But one of the twins woke up. A tinny shriek echoed from their bedroom.

"Come on, Madison," Uncle Roger said from the door. He held the screen open for her. "Don't bother your mother." Madison ran out again.

Aunt Mei got up and came back

with a twin on each forearm. She brought one over to me.

"Don't you want to hold the baby?" she said, and I knew I wasn't allowed to say no.

The baby was small, but soon grew heavy against my arm when no one took it back. I was afraid I'd hurt it. It was much more fragile than a plastic doll, although it was about the same size. I looked into the tight knot of its face. It opened and closed its lipless mouth. It wasn't as pretty as a baby doll either.

I had to sit very still on the sofa. My arms grew stiff from the weight of the baby. Uncle Roger was helping Madison catch fireflies on the lawn. I could hear their laughter through the window.

Mom and Aunt Mei talked and talked. Who knew they could be so interested in the amount of poop the twins pooped into their diapers? They used to talk about Uncle Roger and Dad. Aunt Mei called them "the Lin Boys." She and Mom liked to compare their good and bad points. Sometimes they talked about their own families, who lived far away. They compared the problems of cousins I'd never met. I knew their names only because I'd heard the stories about them. "I married too quickly," Mom said once. "I just wanted to get away from my family. I'm too impulsive."

"You? You're a rock," Aunt Mei said, then laughed.

"Oh, don't call me that," Mom said.

"But it's true! *My* rock!"

I used to like to eavesdrop on Mom and Aunt Mei. I gathered their secrets like breadcrumbs that would lead me from a dark forest someday. However, lately they didn't even try to hide their problems from me. They spoke in front of me as though they thought I should care. I didn't like this feeling, the way they assumed I wanted to be one of them.

The twin in my arms raised a fist and punched its own eye. I thought it would cry. I braced myself, my whole body tensing. Instead, the baby twisted its face in surprise. It tried putting its fist into its mouth.

"Do you want the baby back?" I suggested hopefully.

"You can keep holding her," Aunt Mei said. Her eyes were half-closed. She leaned back in the rocker. She pushed against the floor with her feet so the rocker creaked back and forth, *crik-crik, crik-crik*. "It's okay."

"I think she's hungry," I said.

I was hoping Mom would notice that I'd been holding that baby for a very long time now. I wanted to go play with Madison, but Mom didn't say anything. She picked up the other twin and rocked it in her arms. "Aren't they precious? Aren't they just like little dolls at this age? I almost wanted a third child, but Walter felt two were enough."

"Two is a hell of a lot," Aunt Mei said.

"Walter always gets his way," Mom said. "He pretends to be very easy-going, but in fact he's the opposite. Extremely stubborn. A workaholic. We never do anything anymore. We never go to the city. If there's one thing I've learned about marriage—"

At that moment, Madison came in the front door. Her hands were cupped together, holding a firefly. Madison's black eyes took in everything and revealed nothing. She tossed the bug into the air. It circled through the room, up and down, but I couldn't see its light blink. In the yellow glow of the lamps in the living room, it just seemed like an ordinary insect.

"Madison, cut it out!" Aunt Mei

barked. "What did I say about no horsing around?"

Madison turned on her heels and fled. The screen door slammed shut behind her, and the baby in my arms woke up. It wailed loudly.

Aunt Mei and Mom turned to stare at me. Their eyes fixed on me as if they were surprised to find I was still in the room. I thought they were going to yell at me, but then Aunt Mei burst into laughter. Not her seal-bark laugh, but a new sound, a laugh that honked through her nose. Then Mom laughed, covering her mouth as though she were coughing. She bent at the waist and put her hand on Aunt Mei's arm. Aunt Mei's face turned bright red from laughing.

She honk-honk-honked through her nose and Mom wheezed another laugh into her hand like a sneeze.

"What's so funny?" I asked. I couldn't help but smile because they were laughing so much. But for the life of me, I couldn't figure out why they were laughing at me.

CHAPTER 5

Last year, when Mom and Dad were going through their "difficulties," Dad spent more and more time at work. He came home later and later. Sometimes well after midnight. I was supposed to be asleep, but I'd hear the car pulling into the driveway and then the garage, and then Dad creeping up the stairs. Sometimes he slept on the sofa in the living room.

Once during this period, Aunt Mei brought Madison over to our house to play. Aunt Mei sat in the dining room with Mom while Mom cried. I let our Siberian husky, George, inside the family room, and Madison, Jeremy, and I played Star Wars. We tied a plastic holster across George's back so he could be Chewbacca. That meant Jeremy was Han Solo. There was only one girl in Star Wars, but I let Madison play Princess Leia. She was our guest. Plus I knew that she had to see the speech therapist at school because of her lisp. So I felt generous. That meant I had to be C-3PO, but that was okay because at least he was a droid, which was cooler than being Luke, a boy. In my version, he was smart and bossy, and everyone else had to obey him.

We escaped the trash compactor three times. We were going blow up the Death Star for a second time when Aunt Mei was finally ready to take Madison home. We were sitting on the couch cushions on the floor in X-wing formations. We waved paper-towel-roll light sabers. When we turned around, Mom was standing in the doorway. Her arms were folded across her chest. She wasn't crying anymore, but she wasn't smiling either. She was staring at us playing.

Aunt Mei called through the door, "Hurry up and finish, Madison! We have to go home." And we charged Darth Vader and killed him and then blew up the new Death Star. We ran back and forth across the linoleum. George's paws kept sliding, and he plowed into us, then howled.

We kids all laughed, and even Aunt Mei joined in.

"Come on. Playtime's over," Mom said, her voice flat.

Madison gave me back her light saber. "Auntie Linda, George wath Chewbacca," she lisped.

But Mom wasn't standing in the doorway watching us anymore. She'd already left.

CHAPTER 6

Two weeks before school started, we finally got my bra. First we picked up Jeremy's school stuff from the A&P: crayons and glue and blunt-tipped scissors. At home, Jeremy used regular scissors and even an X-Acto knife, but what did the school know.

After we took everything back home, Mom told Dad to watch Jeremy. "Girls' shopping day," she said. Off Mom and I went, just the two of us.

The training bras at Stern's were hidden in the back, behind the women's slips and the silky pajamas. They were hanging discreetly on a divider between the Lingerie and Hosiery sections.

The light shone from above. The

white polyester of the bras looked even whiter than usual, like an advertisement for bleach. I said, loudly, "Oh, look at the bathrobes." I pointed past the bras to the tangled rack of robes, just in case anyone was watching us, just to throw them.

Mom walked right up to the training bras. She scanned the rows and plucked one from the hanger. Then she held it up to my body to check the size. She pressed the fabric against my blouse, against the flatness of my chest. Right there in the aisle, for the whole world to see.

"Oh my god! Mom!" I exclaimed. Dying, I slipped away into Hosiery. I disappeared into the displays of upturned plaster legs kicking into the air. My heart was pounding, my cheeks burning, and my eyes stung. I blinked and blinked again. All around me were picture after picture of women with their arms crossed over their naked torsos. They were wearing nothing but pantyhose over their long legs in taupe, suntan, nude, and shimmer. It seemed that they were deliberately mocking me as I crouched near the floor. In shame, I pretended to tie my shoelaces.

Fortunately, Mom didn't come looking for me. Or worse, call my name.

I watched from my hiding spot as she found a saleslady to ring up the bra.

I crouched down again and hid. I saw Mom walk away with a silver-and-black Stern's bag under her arm. After a pause, I was going to come out again.

I would wander over to her, casually holding a package of tights, as though that's what I'd come to buy all along. But there weren't any tights for girls. I was in the wrong section entirely. Then I heard Mom's voice rising in laughter.

I hoped none of my friends' mothers were here. I didn't want anyone to find out about this until I'd had time to tell them myself. Humiliation was easier to control that way.

But the next voice wasn't a woman's. It was low and rumbly. A man.

What crazy father would be here in the women's section? I thought. Seriously, not even Mr. Glinbizzi would do that. That's why there were chairs by the elevators. Men waited there for their wives and talked to each other. I'd seen them.

I followed the sound of Mom's voice and found her in the aisle, my Stern's bag still under her arm. She was laughing at something the man was saying. He was wearing a suit jacket, *tweed*. I knew because Dad had one like that, too. But this man was older, with gray in his curly hair, and he was white.

"Linda," he said, and the way he said it made Mom laugh again.

I hurried over. "Hey, Mom," I said, my voice a little too loud in my own ears. "They didn't have any tights in my size." And I bumped into her arm.

"And this must be Jun-li," the man said.

I didn't like that he knew my name.

"That's not how you're supposed to say it," I said. "It's Chinese. It has tones.

Jun. Li." I tried to pronounce it just like Ye-ye and Nai-nai did, loud.

"Oh, Jun-li," Mom said, the way she always did, but the man laughed, so Mom laughed, too.

"Well, it was very nice running into you, Linda," he said.

"Likewise," Mom said. She tucked a strand of hair behind her ear as she spoke. "Jun-li, Tom is a colleague from work. He teaches in the literature department."

Tom, I thought.

"I'll work on those tones," the man said. "JUN LI."

I smiled in a tight way, the way Maria and Cindy and I did when we were being fake polite to girls we didn't like in school. This man didn't seem to notice.

"She's just beautiful," he said to Mom.

And Mom said, "Thank you," as though she'd been the one he was complimenting.

I was in a sour mood the whole drive back home, although Mom didn't say anything more.

I couldn't even look forward to calling Cindy and Maria and telling them about my bra. What could I say?

CHAPTER 7

That night at dinner, Mom was particularly happy. Dad said her spaghetti was delicious and Jeremy asked if he could get another dog. He'd been reading about basset hounds in school and he would like a basset hound.

Dad said, "Absolutely not."

Mom said, "Honey, George will resent another dog."

"I think we should get another dog," I said. The words just fell out of my mouth, surprising me.

Mom and Dad turned to stare. They weren't used to my taking Jeremy's side in anything.

"A basset hound would be nice," I

said. "It could be my dog. I don't have a dog."

"But Jun-li, you'll be too busy. You're starting school in two weeks. And junior high is very different from elementary school," Mom said. She smiled then, but not a nice smile. She said, "Jun-li and I went shopping for junior high today."

And I knew then she was going to mention the training bra. I wouldn't have thought it possible, the betrayal from my own mother. She had the same look in her eye that teachers got when they were going to spring a pop quiz. The look meant business.

"You're right," I said. "I'm going to be too busy. Besides, George will feel bad."

"But Maaa—" Jeremy started, drawing his voice into a whine.

"Listen to Jun-li!" Dad said, saying my name in tones. "Your sister's older. She knows what she's talking about."

Jeremy dropped his chin into his chest. "It's not fair!" he sniffed. Then he pushed his chair back noisily and ran up the stairs.

Dad sighed and continued eating, and Mom turned to me and wrinkled her nose. I knew that was how she winked. It was her own special version because she couldn't quite close only one eyelid at a time. She used to do this when I was younger and she took me to get ice cream on Saturday mornings after grocery shopping. It would just be the two of us, while Jeremy was at home watching cartoons and Dad worked in his study. "Girls have to have their secrets," she'd say, wrinkling her nose.

And automatically, I winked back at her, first my left eye, then my right. That was how I'd practiced in the mirror, over and over till I'd gotten it down.

But that night, I didn't feel happy winking with my mother. Who ever said I'd wanted to have secrets? Whose big idea was that?

There was nothing I could do, however. Secrets were better than telling the embarrassing truth. A girl didn't need to be in junior high to know that.

CHAPTER 8

That night, long after my family had gone to sleep, I lay in my bed reading. I had two books hidden under my pillows—a Trixie Belden mystery and a new Nancy Drew—and a third tucked between the mattress and the wall. Normally I would pull one out as soon as the lights went dark in my parents' room. That was when I knew Mom wasn't going to come back in and tell me to turn off the light. I also kept a flashlight on my dresser for times when Mom stayed up very late.

But Mom was sound asleep and hadn't come creeping through the hall since she went to bed.

That night none of my books could

occupy me. I read a few pages in one, part of a chapter in another, but I could not enter the stories and live with the characters as I usually did. The world outside my books seemed suddenly too noisy. I could hear the faucet dripping in the bathroom and water running through the pipes in the wall. The wind was not particularly strong, but I could hear the maple trees swaying. A few leaves had started to turn yellow. Now I could hear the crisper leaves take flight. They crackled like fire as they fell.

Outside, George was shaking his head. His tags jangled on the collar. He yawned and stretched. I heard his toenails click against the cement of the patio. Then he was off, launched, running through the yard, chasing something in the night.

I lay in bed listening, but I couldn't fall asleep.

Finally, I got up to get a glass of water. While I was standing in the bathroom, Dixie cup in hand, I realized this would be a perfect time to try my bra on. Everyone was still asleep. I tiptoed back to my room and pulled the Stern's bag from under my dresser where I'd hidden it. I pulled the bright-white bra out, ran back to the bathroom, and locked the door.

I pulled my shirt up and slipped my arms through the loops. I had to hook the bra from behind, which was harder than I'd thought. I had to bend over at the waist, my elbows bowed out like wings, till I could slide the hook into the eye.

Then I turned and faced the mirror.

The training bra was white as chalk against my skin. Its lines were like crime-scene outlines across my chest where a bosom was supposed to appear, or worse, had been murdered and taken away. My breath caught in my throat. For a second I wondered if something really was wrong with me. Why were the cups so low? Why did my round belly protrude from beneath my rib cage like a baby's? With the bra in place, I could suddenly see what my body was supposed to look like. I was supposed to look like women on magazine covers in bikinis. But I was nothing like them. Before the bra, I had never even imagined that I was supposed to look like those women. Now I felt odd.

I pulled my pajama top back on over my head. *Maybe the bra will look better under clothes*, I thought. But the effect was even worse. The soft cotton T-shirt no longer lay flat against my skin. Instead, the outlines of the bra showed through the picture of Princess Leia holding her blaster.

Then I heard the noise from downstairs.

CHAPTER 9

What I heard wasn't a breaking or a smashing, but a soft sound. It was like the time George had gotten out of the family room where Mom had put him during a storm. We came back from school and found him. He was in the living room chewing Jeremy's sneakers.

I held my breath and listened. I couldn't hear George running outside anymore, only the wind.

It didn't seem possible he could have gotten in, but I thought I should check. I tiptoed down the hall. I paused at the top of the stairs, listening. Then I stepped onto the first stair, slowly, so that it wouldn't creak. Just in case it wasn't George, but someone else. I wasn't stupid. I knew how to be very quiet. This was how I'd discovered Mom and Dad putting the presents under the tree instead of Santa Claus when I was five. I wasn't like Jeremy, who made noise wherever he went. You had plenty of time to hide things before he arrived.

I crept down, one stair at a time. When I reached the bottom, I crouched and peered around the corner. George wasn't in the living room. It was Dad, stretched out asleep on the sofa.

I stood up.

He shouldn't have been there. He only slept on the sofa when he came home from work late and he didn't want to disturb us by creaking up the stairs.

But he hadn't come home late. And here he was all the same.

I tiptoed to the middle of the living room so that I could see him better. I tiptoed past the piano and right up to the coffee table.

His face was slack. His mouth was turned down. His eyes were puffy-looking without their glasses over them. He lay very still. I wanted to wake him up immediately, the way I had when I was a little girl and I needed something right away. One year I'd gotten up at dawn for Christmas, but Mom said we couldn't open any presents until everyone was awake. Dad slept late on holidays, and by midmorning I couldn't stand the wait. I had filled a glass with cold water and poured it on his face.

He hadn't been angry.

But I didn't dare do that now. I wasn't a little girl anymore. I couldn't pretend I didn't know better.

I crept back to the edge of the staircase and sat at the bottom. My knees bent against my chest, my head rested against my arms, and the tags on my bra scratched at my skin. I didn't even have a book to pass the time, but it didn't matter. The answer I needed wasn't in a book. Instead, I sensed that I should sit, I should be patient. I should wait like this until my father finally woke up.

CHAPTER 10

Shortly after Labor Day, Mom announced that she was separating from our father. "I want you to know this situation has nothing to do with the two of you," she told us. We sat on the couch in the TV room. Jeremy's eyes were wide and scared-looking. "Your father and I love you very much," Mom said.

"I don't want you to go," he managed to say. His eyes filled with tears like a baby's.

"It's because of Tom, isn't it?" I said. I knew it was the man I'd seen in Stern's. I'd kept my ears open when my parents argued. I'd known to listen.

"Jun-li, don't make your brother

upset," Mom said. She sat beside him on the sofa and put her arms around him. He hung his head into her lap and howled. She patted his back. "Look what you've done. Hush, hush."

She rocked with Jeremy in her arms. She acted like he was a baby and not an eight-year-old boy.

I was jealous then. I had to stand there watching my mother comfort him when I wanted to cry, too. What I said was, "I hate you. You can go. You can go forever."

Mom looked up over Jeremy's back. Her eyes narrowed at me, annoyed. "Jun-li, I need you to be reasonable. You're too old to act this way."

I wanted to slap my brother then until his nose bled.

I stole all Jeremy's toy soldiers, the green plastic kind that came in a bag of twenty-five. I threw them in the neighbor's trash. I grabbed his Fantastic Four comic collection and ripped it into shreds. I put salt in his guppy tank and glue on his Legos, but he didn't cry any more and Mom still left Dad.

That fall we moved into the split-level house in Wayne. Tom had had a wife, but they'd gotten a divorce years ago, and they hadn't had kids. His house was smaller than our house, but cleaner. He had many tables with glass tops and glass objects on them that we weren't allowed to touch. Mom said, "I need you two to behave." Mostly we stayed on his lumpy white sectional sofa and watched television, but with the sound down so that we wouldn't annoy him.

Tom was allergic to dog hair, so George had to stay with Dad.

Tom said things like, "I've always wanted children," when he looked at me and Jeremy. Then he smiled by showing his teeth with his lips pulled back, which was not the same thing as just smiling. But I knew the children he'd always wanted were not us. They were his own children.

I thought once Dad finished writing his book, he'd fight to get us back. But every weekend he had the same distracted look on his face. When he did talk to me, he was mostly angry. "Jun-li, finish your plate." And, "Jun-li, what's this B on your science test?" And,

"Don't talk back to me, young lady. You will honor your father and mother!"

I wanted Dad to say, "I don't want you kids living in that strange man's house." And, "I miss you too much when you're away. Please stay with me all the time. We'll figure out how to get your mother back." Or even, "If you stay with me, Mom will miss you too much and have to come back."

But when I talked to him, all I could think to say was, "Dad, this is not how you cook spaghetti." And, "Why are you yelling at me? Jeremy gets Bs all the time and you don't yell at him!" And, "I don't have to listen to you! You don't even live with us anymore!"

Then Dad would shout, "Go to your room, young lady!"

And I'd shout back, "It's not my room! My room is in Tom's house!"

I didn't want to say these things. But after they came out of my mouth, I couldn't take them back. I could only shout louder. I could only pretend I meant everything. And I refused to cry, in front of Dad or Mom or Jeremy or anyone.

CHAPTER 11

Because we'd moved to Wayne, we were too far away to play with our old friends except on Special Occasions. Those were fewer and fewer apart. I was in a new school and didn't have any friends. I was allowed to call Cindy Van Lenten and Maria Glinbizzi on weekends, but they weren't always home. There was a new girl at my old school. She was from Ireland. Her name was Moira. She was all Cindy and Maria could talk about when I called. Moira said this. Moira did that. "You have to meet Moira!" they said. "You'll love her."

I did not want to meet Moira. I knew I would not like her at all.

Mom and I got into more arguments. I didn't clean the house properly. I was lazy. I acted like a princess, sitting and reading when I should be helping. I accidentally broke her favorite teapot when I washed the dishes. I was clumsy. I should be more careful. I made Jeremy upset. I got straight As, but that was only a sign that my school was too easy, Mom said.

Tom said, "Take it easy on her, Linda. She's just a kid, after all."

"You should have seen how I was raised! You should have seen the work I had to do!" And then Tom didn't say anything.

I began to think that Mom wasn't going to be happier with Tom than she had been with Dad, but I didn't know how to say this. Instead, I said nothing.

The next day in school a white boy with red hair and braces smiled at me in the hallway between language arts and lunch. As he passed by, he reached out and snapped the back of my bra.

I could hear the *SNAP* even before I felt it. The sting against my shoulder blades. My back felt on fire, but it was my face that was really burning up with shame.

I turned and he was staring at me, goofy, open-mouthed. Before I knew what I was doing, I swung my three-ring binder right at that face.

I'd never hit anybody before. I

hadn't even aimed, but *pow*! I some-how managed to hit him right in that smirk of his. Unfortunately, he started bleeding on account of his lips hitting his braces.

Naturally, I got detention. The detention monitor, Mrs. Speer, said, "Jun-li, I'm very surprised. What's got-ten into you?"

I couldn't explain it. I could only shrug. But I wasn't sorry I'd hit him. I only pretended to be sorry because I knew that was what adults expected.

CHAPTER 12

In late October, Jeremy's best friend, Seymour, held his birthday party at Greene Lake. Mom let us go because she said Jeremy needed to see his old friends. It would make his adjustment easier. She made me go, too. I would rather have gone to see *my* friends, but Mom said I had to watch Jeremy.

Seymour invited too many kids, his whole class. The school had a new policy: you had to invite everyone or no one. It was a very hot, muggy weekend, as though summer were refusing to end. Everyone showed up at the lake with little sisters and brothers in tow. Parents must have figured this was a good place to dump everyone for an afternoon. It would get them out of the sticky houses, let them blow off steam one last time.

The lake was artificial, not very large, and not very clean. Normally, Mom didn't let us swim there. Jeremy and I had both gotten ear infections the summer we'd gone there for our swim lessons with the Red Cross. That was when I was in second grade. After putting drops in our ears for a week, Mom was sick of it. She only took us to the pool at the Y after that. Then we stayed in the shallow end, since we'd never finished the swim lessons.

Dad let Mrs. Beck take us. Mrs. Beck was happy to have me along because she knew I was dependable. I'd heard her call me this to Mom once.

It meant she could leave the little kids with me and go do other things and I'd have to take care of them.

No one was looking after Jeremy when he and Seymour had a fight on the sand. They were sitting on the bank with their action figures, the Hulk versus the Thing. Seymour threw sand into Jeremy's eyes. I could hear the argument from where I sat with my book. Seymour was used to getting his way. He had a crooked leg and two younger brothers, so his mother spoiled him. Jeremy was usually kind to him, too, but this time Jeremy got up and left.

Out of the corner of my eye I saw his chunky self run across the sand, but I didn't follow. I didn't stop him. I told myself I was too busy looking after the younger kids, who were tossing a beach ball at the edge of the water. In truth, I was angry with Jeremy for being our mother's favorite. I let him go.

Mr. Tralucci was the one who noticed Jeremy had been gone for a while. He had some kind of father's sixth sense.

Then everyone had to get out of the water. We stood in clumps on the artificial beach, on the dirt mixed with imported sand. The adults counted heads, and the lifeguards blew their whistles. Some of the men shouted Jeremy's name. One of the lifeguards jumped into the water and swam to the wooden dock on the other side of the lake.

A hole opened up in my guts then. I crouched, throwing up. I lost the rainbow Jell-O cake that Mrs. Beck had served and my Happy Meal burger and fries. The mess lay on the sand at the edge of the water.

I knew it was my fault. I'd wanted him hurt, and now Jeremy was missing. He didn't know how to swim and he wasn't at the shallow end. He wasn't playing on the sand. Seymour didn't know where he'd gone. No one remembered when they'd seen him last.

I prayed then like they taught us in church. I prayed, "Please, God, let Jeremy be all right. He can have my toys and he can watch any show on TV and I won't tell when he cheats in Monopoly and I will help him with his spelling homework and math, and I won't complain. Please God please-pleaseplease. PleaseGodplease."

There was a sharp whistle. Then more whistles. A shout. The lifeguards were calling to each other.

I couldn't get up. I knelt in the sand next to my vomit. My legs wouldn't hold me.

Then there was happy shouting. Mr. Tralucci and someone else's father were saying, "He's here! He's here!" Then more voices mashed all together. And Mrs. Beck was screaming, a high-pitched squealing sound.

I looked up and everyone was running to the far side of the lake. A lifeguard was standing on the dock, next to a small boat, the kind grown-up couples like to paddle with their feet. Mom never let us go on them.

It turned out Jeremy had climbed in a paddleboat. He'd made it all the way to the middle of the lake. Then his legs had given out, or the current had caught him, and he went around in circles for a while. The boat had drifted along to the far side near the wooden dock where people like to fish. The boat had hit one of the wood posts and gotten stuck.

Jeremy hadn't shouted for help because he was afraid he'd get in trouble.

I was a little angry at him for being so stupid, for saying nothing when he'd heard everyone calling his name. But I was only angry in a relieved kind of way. Until that day I hadn't known it was possible to feel like that, to feel two completely different emotions at the same time.

Afterward I thought: *For sure, now Mom and Dad can't get divorced. They'll have to stay together.* It was so obvious we needed both of them around. But I was wrong.

Dad said this was proof we could survive by ourselves.

I didn't see how he figured it.

But maybe he didn't have a choice. Maybe he just said what he hoped to be true.

Adults, I was learning, could be tricky like that.

CHAPTER 13

After the "Lake Incident," as they called it, Aunt Mei and Uncle Roger invited Dad, Jeremy, and me over to their house for dinner. As she let us in the door, Aunt Mei said, "It's time for you to get on with the rest of your life." I thought this was a funny thing to say.

"We need to cheer up Walter here," she said. "Isn't that right, Roger?"

Uncle Roger was in the kitchen. I could hear things sizzling. "Sit down, sit down," he called. "How ya doing, kids? Sit down, everybody!"

"Ignore the house," Aunt Mei said. It pretty much looked the same as always. There were newspapers on the coffee table and laundry baskets on the furniture and books on the piano bench.

They'd put an extra leaf in the dining room table for us.

The twins were in matching high chairs: one between Aunt Mei and Madison, one between Aunt Mei and Uncle Roger. Both Aunt Mei and Uncle Roger had little plastic bowls of an orange mush and tiny blue spoons. First one twin grabbed a bowl and put it on its head. Then the second one threw its bowl on the floor.

"Not again," Madison said.

At first I could smell the diaper genie in a corner somewhere, although I couldn't see it. But after a while the smell faded away. Uncle Roger had made his famous Sichuan noodles and homemade pickles. Soon everything smelled like peppery steam and oil. The rabbit was now in a cage. Madison said we might be able to let it out to play later if her parents were in a good mood and if the twins went to sleep. She sighed, which made her seem older than nine.

Everyone was acting especially happy for our sake. It made them seem very fake. Aunt Mei joked about setting Dad up with someone else, a woman from her church who played the organ.

Uncle Roger said, "What about one of your students, Walter? That will get Linda's attention."

"Ew," I said, but nobody was listening to me.

Dad said, "No, no, no. We're a

family, the three of us. We need to stick together. We're going to hang out. We're going to have a great time together." He said this in the same flat voice that he'd been speaking in for months. He'd sounded this way long before the Lake Incident, ever since Mom moved out of our house and into Tom's place.

"Can we go to Disneyland?" Jeremy asked.

"No," I said bitterly. I understood these things in a way Jeremy did not. "We have school."

"Maybe we can go somewhere special during your winter break," Dad said.

"Really?" Jeremy said, perking up.

"Yes. I've been invited to present a

paper at an Asian studies conference. I can bring you two along."

"That's not Disneyland." I could not be fooled like Jeremy. I was not a child. I was practically a teenager, after all.

"It's even better," Dad said. "It's in Vancouver. In Canada."

I knew something was up. We never went on trips. Not since I was six or seven and we'd driven up to Vermont to see the fall leaves. It had been Mom's idea, and Jeremy had gotten carsick. We drove five hours back to New Jersey with the windows down to try to blow out the vomit smell.

Dad sighed. "We need to have good times as a family. We need good memories, too," he said in his robot voice.

Aunt Mei and Uncle Roger joined in, their voices shiny as new nickels. "What a great idea, Walter!" said Uncle Roger.

"Sounds like a plan! What a fun trip for you and the kids!" said Aunt Mei.

"Can I get a basset hound?" Jeremy asked, pushing his luck.

"No," said Dad.

So we didn't go to Disneyland, but we did go to the conference with Dad. He was going to deliver a paper from his textbook, *The History of Asians in America*.

I was sure Mom would show up. I thought Dad was plotting something. A surprise reunion. *We're not just doing this, going to this conference with all these*

strangers wearing nametags, I thought.
We're not a family when there's only three.

But Mom wasn't in the Blue Room
reception for Asian studies scholars.
She wasn't waiting at the buffet for conference participants. I went to the buffet three times. I walked back the long
way past all the tables with my plate full
of teriyaki wings and overly dry rice. I
was looking for her. She wasn't on the
bus tour that Dad and Jeremy and I
took through the streets of Vancouver.
She wasn't in the crowd watching the
powwow in the park. Jeremy and Dad
watched the fancy dancers in their
beautiful leather dresses and colorful
shirts, but I scanned the crowd, waiting. I was sure that she would show up.

Dad let Jeremy eat too much candy

and he got a stomachache. We went back to our hotel room early. We did not go to the conference banquet, where professors were giving boring speeches. I had wondered if Dad was going to give a speech, too.

But Dad stayed up with Jeremy. Dad took him back and forth to the bathroom after he started getting sick.

He let me watch TV, and I saw *The Tonight Show Starring Johnny Carson* and then *Love, American Style*. The second show was boring. It was just a bunch of adults talking all the time, but it opened with fireworks over the credits. I knew then how I'd brag about this trip at school. Even though it had been terrible, I couldn't admit that. I was the new girl. I had to show some pride. So when the teachers asked, I'd say, *We went to a conference in Canada and they had fireworks even though it wasn't the Fourth of July*, and I wouldn't be lying.

CHAPTER 14

A year later the divorce was final.

Then Dad's publisher canceled his book. His old editor had moved to a different publishing house and the new editor didn't like it.

I thought Dad would be depressed. I thought it would be like a second divorce, and I was worried.

We had a family dinner in Manhattan for Ye-ye and Nai-nai's anniversary. Mom let Jeremy and me go even though it wasn't Dad's weekend.

Dad drove into the city and picked up Ye-ye and Nai-nai at their apartment. Then he drove us to their favorite restaurant in Chinatown. He let us get out in front of the Gingko Tree while he went to look for parking. I could hear *pop! pop! pop!* from all the tough Chinatown kids setting off firecrackers. It was two weeks before New Year's, but everyone was already setting them off.

"Ye-ye, we need to get some firecrackers," I said. I tugged on his hand.

"It's too dangerous," he said in Chinese. "You could get hurt."

"No, I'm not a little kid anymore," I said in English. I was, in fact, taller than both he and Nai-nai now. I knew that I couldn't just beg. I had to find a good reason. "And it's important. We need to drive away the evil spirits. We need to cheer up Dad. We need to start the year off right."

Ye-ye smiled. His eyes crinkled into his skin. "Where did you hear about evil spirits? There are no evil spirits in America."

"Maybe not in New York, but in New Jersey. When we were in Canada, Dad let us watch the fireworks at night and he seemed happier," I said, which wasn't really a lie.

"Fireworks," Ye-ye said in English, repeating the word. Then he said in Chinese, "When your father was a boy, he used to set off strings of firecrackers for spring festival."

"Yes, we should do that, too," I said. "For good luck."

Ye-ye seemed pleased with the idea. He put his finger over his lips, and said in English, "Don't tell Nai-nai. She will be worried."

I shook my head and crossed my

heart. Ye-ye let Nai-nai take Jeremy inside the Gingko Tree to "hold our table." Then Ye-ye said he and I were going for a walk to get *bao* for dessert.

"Get some *mi tong*, too!" Nai-nai said.

"We will," I promised, and Ye-ye and I set off down the street as though we were headed for Mei Mei's Bakery on Mott Street. But instead we turned a corner and kept walking. Ye-ye said he knew the best place to go. We went down an alley where there were stands set up.

The stands sold flowers in pots and packets of red envelopes and lucky New Year door posters and scrolls of beautiful Chinese writing. Ye-ye kept going until he found a stand that smelled like incense. He talked to the old man in Chinese and the man let us into his shop. There were all kinds of firecrackers and smoke bombs and cherry bombs and bottle rockets and giant rockets. Ye-ye smiled as he discussed the options with the man. In the end, we bought an entire brown bag full of explosives.

Then, just to throw Nai-nai off our trail, we did go to Mei Mei's. We bought pink boxes full of red bean buns and the sweet puffed rice snacks that Nai-nai wanted. We even bought some sesame balls for good measure.

Walking back to the restaurant, Ye-ye held my hand even though I was really too old for that. I didn't mind because it made me feel like his part-ner in crime.

"Jun-li, how did you think of this good idea?" Ye-ye said in English. "This will be the best New Year ever!"

I felt doubly proud. I could've skipped all the way to the Gingko Tree if it wouldn't have been so undignified.

CHAPTER 15

For Chinese New Year, Dad invited everyone over: Uncle Roger, Aunt Mei, Madison and the twins, Ye-ye and Nai-nai. Mom stayed with Tom of course, but for once Mom and Dad didn't fight about who got us when and how long we'd stay. Tom was white and this was not his holiday but *ours*, so we had the right to go, no arguments.

Ye-ye brought out the firecrackers and smoke bombs. He said to Dad in Chinese, "This was Jun-li's idea. You can show her what you used to do."

Nai-nai was inside, cooing over the twins, so there was no one to stop us from starting.

Dad showed Jeremy and me how

to throw bang snaps against the patio in the backyard. Then he taught us how to set off the smoke bombs. They twirled in circles and then shot out colored smoke—orange and blue and yellow. Then the cherry bombs and the sparklers.

Then Dad saw the extra-big rocket. Ye-ye had purchased it for the finale.

"You're the oldest, Jun-li," he said. "You better light it." Dad gave me a wink.

Jeremy said, "No fair!" but Dad said, "When you're older, Jeremy." He handed me the giant matchstick and held the launcher steady as I applied the flame to the long, trailing fuse.

The rocket took off with an actual *whoosh!* sound. It shot away so fast that we couldn't follow it with our eyes. Jeremy and Uncle Roger and I crouched in the grass, wondering where it had gone. Dad stood scanning the sky. Then, all of a sudden, we heard a *BOOM!* like thunder. A giant white ball of flame like a small sun appeared over the roof. "Ooooh!" we cried. And then the sun disappeared just as quickly. It exploded into tiny points of light. The lights circled and spun through the dark sky like a million drunken fireflies.

"Ahhh!" we sighed as the lights fell in dotted lines to the ground.

"That better not cause a fire," Aunt Mei said. "You better make sure nothing is burning. I'm pretty sure that one was against the law."

So Dad grabbed some flashlights from the garage, where we'd locked George for the night. We each had one—Jeremy, me, Madison, Dad, Uncle Roger, and even Aunt Mei. It was too cold for Ye-ye, so he went indoors to watch the twins with Nai-nai.

We all ran through the backyard. We shone our flashlights across the grass, into the shrubs and up through the branches of the trees. Our bodies were invisible in the dark, but our beams of light showed pieces of the yard in bursts. A tree. A shrub. George's dog bowl. Branches of the elm tree. The baseball we lost last summer and couldn't find again until now.

As we were running in the cold February air, I could hear Dad and

Uncle Roger panting. They sounded like horses or large dogs. Jeremy and Madison were giggling. "Bzzz, bzzz!" they called out, pretending to cross light sabers. Aunt Mei ran into a tree and swore out loud. We never found any sparks in the grass, but our house didn't burn down either, so the rocket must have burnt out in the sky.

Later, we all laughed in the kitchen. Our cheeks were red from the cold. Dad made us hot tea to warm up.

Ye-ye said in Chinese, "This New Year will bring good luck for all of us!"

Aunt Mei said, "We'll be lucky if the neighbors don't call the police on us."

Dad said, "Well, this was the first and last time. They might not be so forgiving next year. But Ye-ye's right. This was a good idea, Jun-li!" He looked so happy. I felt very proud. Yes, me and my good idea.

However, it was *not* the last time, and the firecrackers became a family tradition. They weren't technically legal in New Jersey. We kept the following year's celebration small and close to the ground, mostly sparklers and smoke bombs. In fact, Ye-ye didn't buy any big rockets again until Jeremy's high school graduation, but that is another story.

I used to wonder what would have happened if we'd set off fireworks earlier, when Mom was still married to Dad. If we'd gone running together in the backyard every holiday, looking for sparks to put out, maybe they would have stayed together. It had been so much fun. I think Mom would have liked it.

But Maria Glinbizzi and Cindy Van Lenten said no, you couldn't predict things with adults. They did what they wanted. Fun or not, they had their own ideas. Who could understand them?

I had to agree. By then we were fourteen, teenagers. I'd grown four inches over the summer. I was taller than Aunt Mei. Someday soon I'd outgrow my mother. Everything about my mother seemed smaller.

At fourteen, we knew all that we wanted to know about adults. And the three of us promised, sharing a cigarette that Maria had stolen from her mother's purse: We would not be like them when we grew up. Not ever.

ACKNOWLEDGMENTS

I would like to thank Penelope Dane and Gwynn Gacosta for reading multiple drafts of stories about these characters; Allison Grimaldi-Donahue at *Queen Mob's Tea House* for publishing a story about some of these characters in a different timeline; Trish O'Hare, publisher of Gemma Open Door for this opportunity to create a multicultural text for people learning to read in English; Jennifer Sale for her judicious copyediting; and to my family for their love and support (and fireworks): Winberg Chai and Jeff, Virginia, Ariel, Everett, Adelaide, and Evelyn Chai.